Contents

The
Dead of Night

Brandon Robshaw

Published in association with
The Basic Skills Agency

Hodder & Stoughton

A MEMBER OF THE HODDER HEADLINE GROUP

Acknowledgements
Cover: Darren Hopes
Illustrations: Chris Coady

Orders: please contact Bookpoint Ltd, 130 Milton Park, Abingdon, Oxon OX14
4SB. Telephone: (44) 01235 827720. Fax: (44) 01235 400454. Lines are open from
9.00–6.00, Monday to Saturday, with a 24 hour message answering service.
You can also order through our website www.hodderheadline.co.uk.

British Library Cataloguing in Publication Data
A catalogue record for this title is available from the British Library

ISBN 0 340 87667 0

First Published 2003
Impression number   10 9 8 7 6 5 4 3 2 1
Year   2007 2006 2005 2004 2003

Typeset by Fakenham Photosetting Limited, Fakenham, Norfolk
Printed in Great Britain for Hodder & Stoughton Educational, a division of
Hodder Headline, 338 Euston Road, London NW1 3BH by Athenaeum
Press Ltd.

1
The Dead of Night

Edinburgh, 1853.
It was the dead of night.
There was no moon.
Only the yellow light of gas lamps.
A church clock struck two.

A horse and cart
rattled through the dark streets.
Two men sat in it.
Mr Brown
and Mr Harker.

Brown was a large, fat man
with a beard.
Harker was small and thin
with sharp eyes.
He held the reins.

It was a cold night.
Their breath came out
in clouds of steam.

The cart climbed up the hill.
They left the city centre behind.
It got darker.
There were not so many gas lamps now.
Soon they would be
at the graveyard.
Soon they would be
at work.

2
Work

'It will be a good night tonight,'
said Harker.
'Six buried today.
I know where the graves are.
I was at the funerals.'

Brown didn't answer for a bit.
Then he said,
'I don't like this work.'

'No one likes their work,' said Harker.
'But it's a living.'

Brown and Harker were grave-robbers.
They dug up bodies from graves.
They sold them
to Edinburgh Medical School.

They sold them to Dr Black.
He needed bodies to teach his students.
The students cut them up.
It was part of their training.
They had to know
what a human body
looked like inside.

Brown and Harker never told Dr Black
where the bodies came from.
He never asked.
What they were doing
was against the law.
That was why they had to work
in the dead of night.

The horse and cart
rattled round a bend.

Ahead they saw
the iron gates of the graveyard.

They saw something else, too.
Something they weren't expecting.

'Oh, no!' said Harker.

3

The Policeman

A policeman stood outside
the graveyard.
He wore a thick coat.
He carried a lantern.
In his other hand,
he held a long stick.

'Damn,' said Harker.
He pulled the reins and the horse stopped.
'They've put a policeman on guard.
Someone must have noticed
the graves were being dug up.
Now what are we going to do?'

'Well, we can't rob any graves tonight,'
said Brown.
'Not with him there.'
He was not sorry.
He hated robbing graves.
He hated the sight of dead people.
They scared him.
He hated the smell of them, too.
It made him feel sick.

But, as Harker said,
it was a living.

'We must think of a plan,'
said Harker.

'Let's go for a drink,'
said Brown.

4
The Inn

They found an inn
that was still open.
It was in the centre of town.
It was not very crowded.
Most people were in bed by now.
There were just
a few tired old drunks left.

Brown and Harker stood at the bar.
Harker ordered two whiskies.
'So, what are we going to do?'
he asked.

'I don't know.
We can't get into the graveyard.
Maybe we should give up.
Find another way
to make a living.'

Harker shook his head.
'I don't think so.'

He leaned forward
and whispered in Brown's ear,
'Look at all these old men in here.
Drunk. No use to anyone.
In a year or two
they'll all be dead.'

'What are you saying?' asked Brown.

'In a year or two
they'll be in the graveyard,'
said Harker.
'Why wait for them to get there?'

12

'You mean—?'

'Look at that wee fellow there,'
said Harker.

Brown looked.
The old man was small and weak.
He kept coughing.
He had no teeth.
He was drunk.
His face was red.

'What use is that man to anyone?'
said Harker.
'It would be an act of mercy
to put him out of his misery.'

Brown looked unhappy.
'Well – I don't know ...'

Just then the old man finished his drink.
He staggered to his feet.
He staggered to the door.

'Come on!' said Harker.
'Let's follow him!'

5
A Good Deed

They followed the old man
down the street.
He was swaying from side to side.

'I don't like this,' said Brown.
'What are we going to do?'

'Don't fret,' said Harker.
'We're just earning our living.
We'll finish the old man off.'

'But that's not right!'

'Of course it's right!
He's no use to anyone.
He'll be more use when he's dead,
teaching students to be doctors.
We're doing a good deed!'

They followed him
through the dark, empty streets.
They were only a few steps behind.
The old man turned
into a dark alley.

'Time for our good deed,' said Harker.

6
Murder

They followed him into the alley.
They grabbed him
and pushed him against the wall.
The old man cried out in terror.

'Hush your noise,' said Harker.
'This won't hurt much.'

The old man stared at them.
'Who are you? What do you want?'

'It won't take a minute.
Brown, give us your scarf.'

'What for?'

'Just hand it over!'

Harker took Brown's thick, woollen scarf.
The old man began to scream.
He stopped as Harker pressed the scarf
over his nose and mouth.

Harker held the scarf there
for a long time,
pressing hard.
The old man struggled for a while,
then went limp.

Harker let go.
The old man fell to the ground.

'Is he – is he dead?' asked Brown.

'Oh, aye, he's dead all right,'
said Harker.
'Let's get him back to the cart.'

7

Helping him Home

'Help me pick him up,' said Harker.
'We'll carry him between us.
It will look as if he's drunk
and we're helping him home.'

They put his arms around their shoulders.
They walked him back to
their horse and cart.
They passed no one.

'I don't like this,' said Brown.
'We should never have done it.
It's not right.'

'Hush,' said Harker.
'Think how pleased Dr Black will be.
And think how pleased
we'll be to get our money!'

They loaded the old man's body
into the back of the cart.
Then they climbed up
and Harker took the reins.
They rattled along
the dark, empty streets,
by the side of the river.

'Let's hope there's no police around,'
said Brown.
'We don't want to be stopped.'

'Don't fret!' said Harker.
'There's nothing to worry about.'

Then he shouted in terror.
A hand grabbed him by the shoulder.

8
Into the River

Brown shouted too.
A hand had grabbed his shoulder as well.
Both men turned round.

The face of the old man
was grinning out from the back
of the cart.
His eyes were dead,
but his mouth curved up
in a toothless grin.

He had one hand on each man's shoulder
and his face grinned between them.
His grip tightened.

Brown fainted.
Harker swore and pulled at the reins.
The horse swerved to one side.
The cart went off the road
and tumbled into the river.

The cold water hit Harker
like a knife.
He struggled to come to the surface.
The old man's hand
was holding him under.

Harker couldn't breathe.
He opened his mouth
and felt the ice-cold water
pour into his lungs.

9
Medical School

—————

'Watch closely, gentlemen,' said Dr Black.
He was standing in the lecture theatre
of Edinburgh Medical School.
A group of students stood around him.

'Today we have two bodies to look at.
They were found drowned in the river.'

The bodies lay on a table.
They were covered with a sheet.
Dr Black pulled back the sheet.

He gave a start of surprise.
He knew these men,
Brown and Harker.
They had often sold him bodies.
Now they were bodies themselves
on his operating table.
It was strange.

Well, they were dead now
and life had to go on.
He picked up his knife.

'Watch closely, gentlemen,
as I cut open the chest...'